Sid

Written by Hatty Skinner
Illustrated by Hannah Wood

Collins

Dip in tins.

Sid naps.

mat

Dad pads in.

Sid sits.

Nip a man.

Sid naps.

mat

Dad pads in.

Sid sits.

man

Pans tip.

mat

11

Pam did it.

Dad pats Sid.

/i/

6

14

After reading

Letters and Sounds: Phase 2

Word count: 36

Focus phonemes: /s/ /a/ /t/ /p/ /i/ /n/ /m/ /d/

Curriculum links: Personal, social and emotional development

Early learning goals: Reading: read and understand simple sentences; use phonic knowledge to decode regular words and read them aloud accurately

Developing fluency

- Your child may enjoy hearing you read the book.
- Take turns to read two pages. Check your child pauses between sentences and does not forget to read the labels.

Phonic practice

- Turn to page 2 and sound out each word together. (*D/i/p i/n t/i/n/s*) Ask: Which word has the /d/ sound?
- On page 4, focus on the /d/ and /p/ sounds. Read the sentence together. Ask your child: Which words have the /d/ sound? (**Dad** *and* **pads**) Which word has the /p/ and /d/ sounds? (**pads**)
- Look at the "I spy sounds" pages (14 and 15). Point to and sound out the /i/ at the top of page 14, then point to the igloo and say "igloo", emphasising the /i/ sound. Take turns to find an item in the picture that starts with or contains the /i/ sound. (*ink, bin, six, cricket, insects, pink, drink, Sid, dig, sit*)

Extending vocabulary

- Turn to pages 4 and 5 and read the label. Discuss why Sid is **sad**. Point to Dad and ask: How do you think Dad is feeling? (e.g. *cross, angry*). Look through the book and discuss what "feeling" words could be added to the pictures. (e.g. *upset, hungry, sleepy, bad, guilty*)